LITTLE MISS WHOOPS

Roger Hargreaves

Written and illustrated by
Adam Hargreaves

Little Miss Whoops is one of those people who have accidents all of the time.

She has lots of little accidents, like when she is trying to make lunch and drops the eggs!

Whoops!

And she has big accidents, like when she painted her bedroom and tripped over the paint pot!

Whoops!

Every morning when she makes her cup of tea, she spills the milk, tips over the sugar bowl, drops the teabag, breaks the biscuits, knocks her cup of tea across the table and has to start all over again.

Whoops!

Some days it can take hours before she leaves the house.

Little Miss Whoops really is the most accidental person in the world . . . well not quite.

Little Miss Whoops has a brother, Mr Bump. He is just like his sister, if not worse, but that is another story. (Which you may have read.)

Each year, Little Miss Whoops travels by train to visit her brother for a week.

She set off last Tuesday.

This Tuesday, Mr Bump looked at his clock.

Which was lying on the ground where he had just knocked it over.

His sister was late.

A whole week late!

And why was Little Miss Whoops late?

A whole chapter of accidents, of course!

While her train was waiting in a station, she somehow or other tripped and fell out of the train.

Whoops!

And then she somehow or other tripped and fell into the back of a lorry, which took her to Sea Town.

Whoops!

Where, somehow or other she tripped and fell into a boat which took her to another country.

Whoops!

She had to wait nearly a week to get another boat
back . . .

. . . and another lorry . . .

. . . and another train.

Little Miss Whoops was exhausted by the time she finally reached her brother's house.

"I thought you were coming last week," said Mr Bump. "It must have been a long trip."

"It was!" said Little Miss Whoops.

"Would you like a cup of tea?" offered Mr Bump.

And you know what that involved don't you?

They spilt the milk, tipped over the sugar bowl, dropped the tea bags, broke the biscuits and knocked the tea all over the table!

What a mess!

Whoops!

"Oh! Look at the time," cried Little Miss Whoops, knocking over the clock. "I've got to go if I'm to catch my train home!"

She grabbed her suitcase and rushed out of the door.

"Goodbye," she called.

"Goodbye," called back Mr Bump. "See you next year!"

Mr Bump waved from the doorway until she had rounded the corner.

Then he closed the door, but as he did, the door handle came off in his hand!

"Whoops!" said Mr Bump.

3 Sixteen Beautiful Fridge Magnets – any 2 for £2.00!
inc.P&P

They're very special collector's items!
Simply tick your first and second* choices from the list below
of any 2 characters!

1st Choice
- [ ] Mr. Happy
- [ ] Mr. Lazy
- [ ] Mr. Topsy-Turvy
- [ ] Mr. Bounce
- [ ] Mr. Bump
- [ ] Mr. Small
- [ ] Mr. Snow
- [ ] Mr. Wrong

- [ ] Mr. Daydream
- [ ] Mr. Tickle
- [ ] Mr. Greedy
- [ ] Mr. Funny
- [ ] Little Miss Giggles
- [ ] Little Miss Splendid
- [ ] Little Miss Naughty
- [ ] Little Miss Sunshine

2nd Choice
- [ ] Mr. Happy
- [ ] Mr. Lazy
- [ ] Mr. Topsy-Turvy
- [ ] Mr. Bounce
- [ ] Mr. Bump
- [ ] Mr. Small
- [ ] Mr. Snow
- [ ] Mr. Wrong

- [ ] Mr. Daydream
- [ ] Mr. Tickle
- [ ] Mr. Greedy
- [ ] Mr. Funny
- [ ] Little Miss Giggles
- [ ] Little Miss Splendid
- [ ] Little Miss Naughty
- [ ] Little Miss Sunshine

*Only in case your first choice is out of stock.

--- TO BE COMPLETED BY AN ADULT ---

**To apply for any of these great offers, ask an adult to complete the coupon below and send it with
the appropriate payment and tokens, if needed, to MR. MEN CLASSIC OFFER, PO BOX 715, HORSHAM RH12 5WG**

- [ ] Please send ____ Mr. Men Library case(s) and/or ____ Little Miss Library case(s) at £5.99 each inc P&P
- [ ] Please send a poster and door hanger as selected overleaf. I enclose six tokens plus a 50p coin for P&P
- [ ] Please send me ____ pair(s) of Mr. Men/Little Miss fridge magnets, as selected above at £2.00 inc P&P

Fan's Name _____

Address _____

_____ **Postcode** _____

Date of Birth _____

Name of Parent/Guardian _____

Total amount enclosed £ _____

- [ ] **I enclose a cheque/postal order payable to Egmont Books Limited**
- [ ] **Please charge my MasterCard/Visa/Amex/Switch or Delta account** (delete as appropriate)

Card Number

Expiry date ___/___   **Signature** _____

MR.MEN   LITTLE MISS
Mr. Men and Little Miss™ & ©Mrs. Roger Hargreaves

CUT ALONG DOTTED LINE AND RETURN THIS WHOLE PAGE